SUPER SPORTS STORIES

TAO'S TOUCHDOWN PASS

by Blake Hoena
illustrated by Christos Skaltsas

GRASSHOPPER

Tools for Parents & Teachers

Grasshopper Books enhance imagination and introduce the earliest readers to fiction with fun storylines and illustrations. The easy-to-read text supports early reading experiences with repetitive sentence patterns and sight words.

Before Reading

- Discuss the cover illustration. What do readers see?
- Look at the glossary together. Discuss the words.

Read the Book

- Read the book to the child, or have him or her read independently.
- "Walk" through the book and look at the illustrations. Who is the main character? What is happening in the story?

After Reading

- Prompt the child to think more. Ask: As quarterback, Tao is a leader on the football team. How does he show leadership?

Grasshopper Books are published by Jump!
5357 Penn Avenue South
Minneapolis, MN 55419
www.jumplibrary.com

Library of Congress Cataloging-in-Publication Data

Names: Hoena, B. A., author. | Skaltsas, Christos, illustrator.
Title: Tao's touchdown pass / by Blake Hoena; illustrated by Christos Skaltsas.
Description: Minneapolis, MN: Jump!, Inc., [2024]
Series: Super sports stories | Includes index.
Audience: Ages 7-10.
Identifiers: LCCN 2022048394 (print)
LCCN 2022048395 (ebook)
ISBN 9798885243971 (hardcover)
ISBN 9798885243988 (paperback)
ISBN 9798885243995 (ebook)
Subjects: CYAC: Leadership–Fiction. | Football–Fiction.
LCGFT: Sports fiction. | Readers (Publications)
Classification: LCC PZ7.H67127 Tao 2024 (print)
LCC PZ7.H67127 (ebook)
DDC [Fic] –dc23
LC record available at https://lccn.loc.gov/2022048394
LC ebook record available at https://lccn.loc.gov/2022048395

Editor: Eliza Leahy
Direction and Layout: Anna Peterson
Illustrator: Christos Skaltsas

Printed in the United States of America at Corporate Graphics in North Mankato, Minnesota.

Table of Contents

Play Hard and Have Fun

Tao looks at the scoreboard. His team, the Ravens, is losing to the Lions. But the Ravens have the ball and one last chance to score.

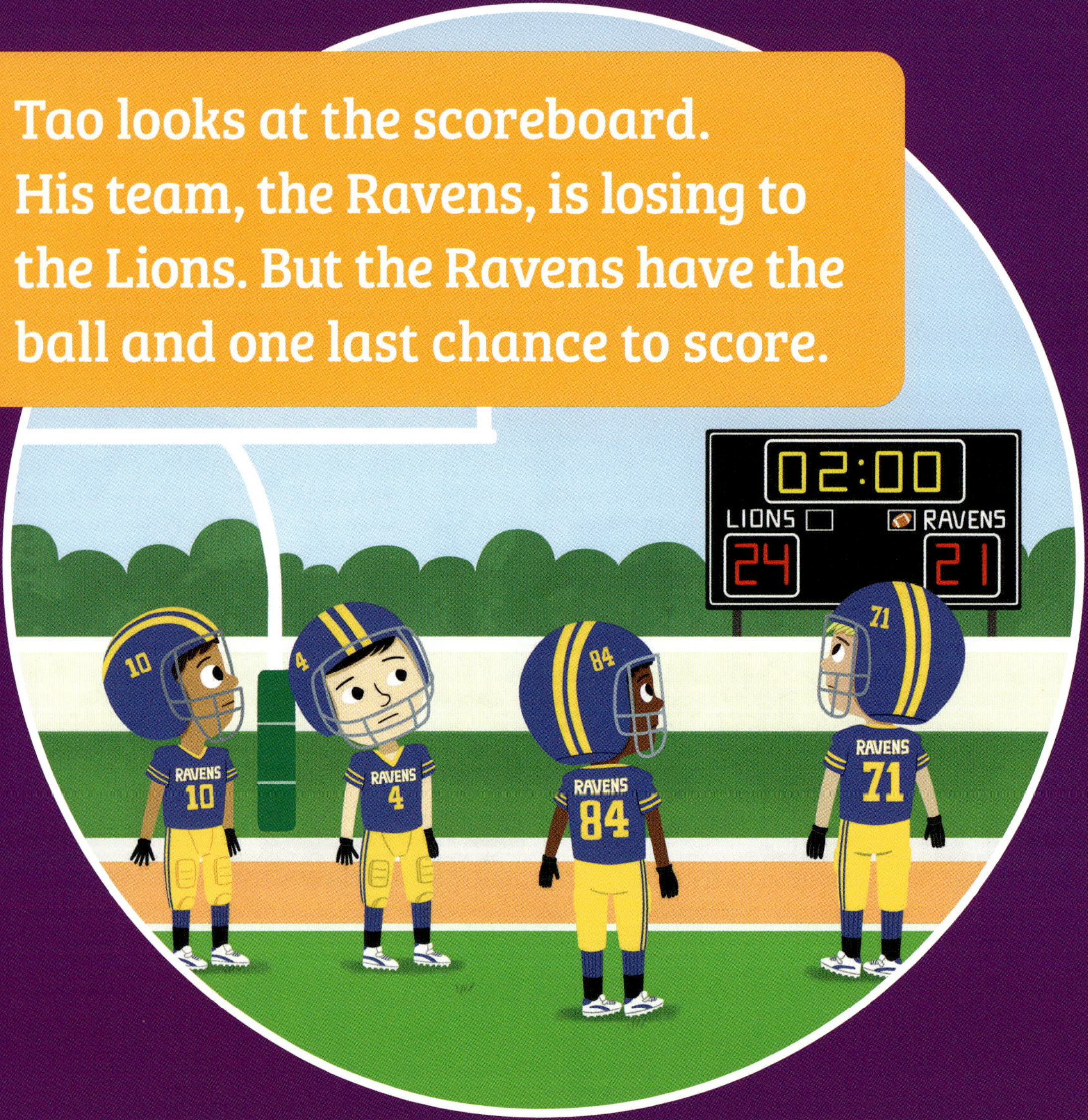

“We only have two minutes left,” Jeremy says. “I don’t know if we can win this one.”

“That doesn’t mean we can’t try!” Tao says. “And we need you. You’re our best receiver.”

"OK, team, huddle up!" Coach Mike shouts. "The game is not over yet, so let's play hard and have fun! One, two, three . . ."

"Go Ravens!" the team yells.

RAVENS
84
4
15
10
9
7
11
52
RAVENS
9
RAVENS
7
RAVENS
1
52
RAVENS
11

"Remember, Tao, as quarterback, it's your responsibility to lead the team," Coach says.

"Got it, Coach," Tao replies. He and the rest of the Ravens' offense run onto the football field.

"Huddle up!" Tao says. His teammates gather around. "First play is going to be a pass." Turning to Jeremy, Tao adds, "I'll be looking for you to get open."

"I'll try," Jeremy says.

They line up, and Tao stands behind the center.

“Ready, set… hike!” Tao calls out.

The center snaps the ball to Tao. Tao steps back to pass. He sees Jeremy running. He throws the ball.

RAVENS
84
LIONS
42

Jeremy reaches for the football.
But it slips through his fingers.
It is an incomplete pass.

Jeremy's shoulders slump as he runs back to the huddle.

"Sorry, guys," he says. "I messed up."

"It's OK. The game isn't over yet," Tao says.

During the next play, Tao looks for an open receiver. He sees Jeremy slowly running.

What is he doing? Tao wonders. But it is too late for him to throw the ball.

WHAM! A defender sacks him.

84
11
34
RAVENS
5
22
10
3
10
6
LIONS
42

The team gets back in a huddle.

"You have to keep trying!" Tao says to Jeremy.

"I don't want to mess up again," Jeremy says.

"Remember what Coach said. Play hard and have fun," Tao says. "It's only fun if we all try our best."

4
84
52
9
VENS
RAVENS
4
RAVENS
84
RAVENS
RAVENS
15
RAVENS
9

On the next play, Tao doesn't have time to look for an open receiver. The Lions' defenders rush toward him. Just before he gets sacked, Tao throws the ball to Jeremy.

Jeremy sees the ball sailing through the air. He races ahead of the defenders. He catches it!

He runs into the end zone.
Touchdown!

Tao and the rest of the Ravens celebrate the team's win.

"I knew you could do it!" Tao tells Jeremy.

"*We* did it!" Jeremy says.

00:02
LIONS
RAVENS
24
27
RAVENS 10
RAVENS 4
RAVENS 52
RAVENS 22
RAVENS 1
RAVENS 7
RAVENS 71

Let's Review!

Tao plays quarterback. What are the offensive positions on a football team? Take a look!

1. **center:** Hikes the ball to the quarterback.
2. **left and right guards:** Line up on either side of the center. They block defenders and protect the quarterback.
3. **left and right tackles:** Line up outside the guards. They block defenders and protect the quarterback.
4. **quarterback:** Leads the team's offense and throws the ball.
5. **running backs:** Mostly rush, or run, with the ball.
6. **tight end:** Lines up outside the tackles. Tight ends are blockers and receivers.
7. **wide receivers:** Mostly catch passes from the quarterback.

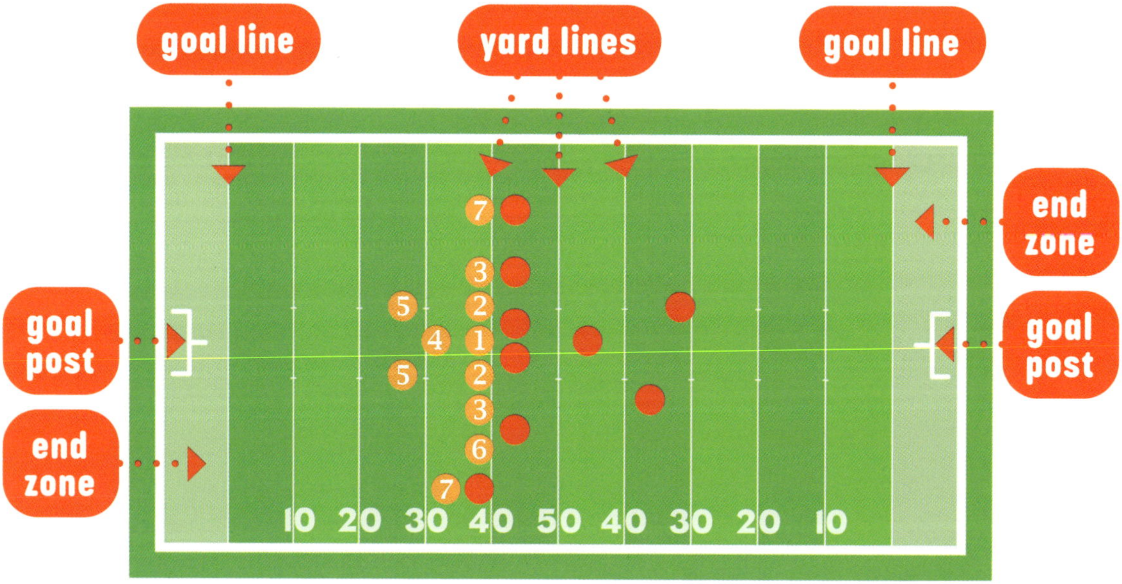

Football Equipment

What equipment does Tao need to play football? Take a look!

To Learn More

Finding more information is as easy as 1, 2, 3.

1. Go to www.factsurfer.com
2. Enter "**Tao'stouchdownpass**" into the search box.
3. Choose your book to see a list of websites.

Glossary

defender: A player whose job is to keep the other team from scoring.

end zone: The area at the end of a football field.

hike: To snap, or pass, the football to the quarterback.

huddle: To crowd together.

incomplete pass: A pass that is not caught.

offense: The part of a football team whose job is to score.

responsibility: A duty or job.

sacks: Tackles the quarterback.

touchdown: A six-point score made by carrying the football into the end zone or catching it in the end zone.

Index